HOW I BECAME A PHONE SEX OPERATOR
MY TRU

Elain

Notes:

HOW I BECAME A PHONE SEX OPERATOR
MY TRUE STORY

Friends and family all know me as Elaine. That's the real me. They don't know I'm also Gabriela the stripper, Angel the mature sex siren and Bridget, the horny housewife married to a cuckold. Those are my phone sex characters. Lately I've even added myself, using my own pictures and life. Think it's easy being 4 people? You try it.

My life has been quite ordinary. I am the youngest of 3 kids. My mother was overloaded due to the early death of her mom. Besides taking care of my siblings and me, she took care of her brothers and dad. I was often told to play outside so she could clean the house. Nothing shocking but it left me wanting attention. I craved it.

I had friends growing up but usually only one close one at a time. My favorite memories are of me playing outside with the boys. No, not sex games. I was shy like a mouse but somehow with my male friends I wasn't. I always preferred playing with the boys. I didn't have a Barbie and I didn't play those girlie games. Instead, the guys and I played super heroes. They were superman and I was supergirl. I adapted.

My first love was a childhood crush on a boy named Danny. Too bad it was one-sided. With him, I was reserved. He was in a car accident and had to wear a cast for a while. I was too timid to look down at his exposed body parts when I visited him at home. He definitely wasn't covered up much by the bandage. Now, I sure would have looked, but at that time I didn't.

I must have been 8 years old but I was hooked on him. Many times I asked his brother Joey, to ask Danny to join us when we played. Danny was cute but he used to ask me how I did in exams, when we were in the same class. I should have lied. My marks were better than his and he would sigh when I told him my grade. Then he'd leave. I wished he didn't ask how I did but he kept doing that. Oh well.

Years later, Danny went to the prom with someone else. I was devastated. A friend of mine asked him why he didn't go with me. Know what his answer was? My boobs weren't big enough. He picked a woman with the biggest tits in class. She was the oldest and had the most developed breasts of all of us girls. He should have waited. My breasts are 40DD. Good things come to those that wait, Danny.

I got asked out a few times by guys but I was never the type to go out just for the sake of it. That might have been a mistake. It just wasn't worth the stress of going out with a guy that didn't interest me. I was very shy.

I worked at summer jobs to make money for school. In Montreal after high school, I went to Cegep. That's the college equivalent there. It was in the summer of 1976 that I went for an interview for the Montreal Summer Olympics. My friends all applied but I ended up with the best job of all of us. The interviewer loved my red hair and I was hired.

My job was working with the Press. They stayed at the Universite de Montreal residences, to write stories for their newspapers about the Olympics. That was where I was situated for my work for the Olympics. I was a Facsimile Operator (early fax machine) and Acceptance Clerk. I had a cute skirt and nice sweater that showed off my now ample breasts. It was there that I met my first boyfriend.

John was my supervisor. He worked for the military reserve while attending University to become an engineer. COJO (Olympic committee) brought in the military to help out. At the end of his first week, he asked me to stay after work. I thought, what did I do wrong? Everyone left and there I was, alone with my boss. He told me to come over to his desk and I did. He asked me if I'd like to go out with him. I was taken aback but I felt something just standing next to him. My body tingled. I wasn't sure what it meant but I sure liked the feeling. I quickly said yes and we ended up going to a restaurant.

John was still in his uniform and it's true, there's nothing like a man in uniform. That is, except a man taking it off. No it didn't happen that first night. It was my first date ever and I was 17 and he was 24. He took my hand and held it at dinner. We went to a movie later and as he said many times afterwards, I probably only said 2 words all night. I made up for it in later dates. After the movie, we went to a coffee shop. He rubbed one of his fingers all over my slightly sweaty palm and I was so horny I couldn't believe it. He stirred up feelings in me that I had no idea I had. When he kissed me good night, I knew I was in love.

I was always the "good girl" who did the right thing. I got good grades, listened to teachers and my parents. Meeting John changed that, not drastically but a bit. No, I didn't become a party girl or take drugs or anything like that. I did however show up late once or twice to work and later ran away to be with him.

John and I used to go up in the mountains and pet. It was right in back of the university and we'd walk around for a spot and lie down. He'd reach over and touch my large breasts and we'd passionately kiss. I only gently rubbed the top of his pants, feeling his aroused cock. I was a virgin. John talked about how beautiful it is when two people made love but I wasn't ready for that yet.

One time my blouse was off and he was touching my tits. We heard someone coming and he threw my shirt at me and told me to put it on quickly. That sure ruined the mood. The fact we almost got caught made it all the more thrilling on subsequent outings. We fondled each other in parks, on grass near my house and anywhere else we could find. That summer was the best and worst in my life. It would have been fantastic had it not been for 2 things, my parents and his job.

My parents liked my boyfriend but had personal reasons that made it impossible for them to accept him being anything more than friends with me. His job almost had him imprisoned for putting his arms around me. Seems military personnel aren't allowed to be cozy with civilians while they're in uniform. The "us against the world" situation we faced, made me want him all the more. When he went back to his life in Ottawa after the Olympics, I went with him. First I stayed at the YMCA. He would sneak in at night and we touched each other but still never consummated our sexual relationship. Later, I came to stay with him and his parents.

Towards the end of the summer, I was about to leave to go back to Montreal and school. He had always told me that he wanted to make love to me. Before I left to go home, I decided it was time to have sex with him and told him so. That way he would have something to remember me by after I left. His face lit up. I was in his brother's bedroom. His brother was sent to another room to sleep, during the few weeks I was there. Located next door to his parents, I lost my virginity.

We stood beside the bed and John kissed me tenderly. Slowly he removed my clothes including my bra and panties and dropped them to the floor. He started licking my pink nipples, which were easily aroused by seeing him look at me. They were erect and hard and ready for the love bite that followed. I shyly touched his shoulders and moved my hands slowly over his jeans, feeling the stirring within. He quickly unzipped and removed his pants and underwear and took off his shirt, adding to the heap on the carpet. John, the man I loved with all my heart, stood in front of me. I looked at his disrobed body and stared at his rising cock. I had never seen anyone's dick before but something about it made me excited. My pussy pulsated for the first time. He held me tight for a moment, sensing my passion mixed with fear of the unknown.

Before I knew it, our naked bodies lay down on the bed but not the way I expected. He inched his growing cock over to my closed mouth and his face was by my now moist pussy. Suddenly he said to me "Suck my cock". I was terrified actually. I had no idea how to do it. That evening was the first time I had seen a prick, let alone put one in my mouth. I stared at it and somehow managed to figure out what to do. I was awkward doing it but he seemed to enjoy it. I slowly moved my timid tongue along his perked up shaft and moistened his engorged cockhead. It looked so big and as I lightly licked it, his uprising dick got increasingly harder. That only added to the wetness in my dampening slit.

"Take it in your mouth," he said. I did as instructed, not sure how much to open my mouth at first. The thick tip of his manhood went gently into my warm passageway, followed by his thick shaft. Inch by inch I took in as much as I could, until I gagged. I couldn't deep throat him then but I could have now. He was making noises that I could tell meant I was pleasuring him. The most important thing to me was making him feel good. It made me happy to know I was succeeding.

When his salivating tongue started deeply licking into my blossoming cunt lips, I softly moaned. It felt strange yet wonderful, to experience his exploring tongue all over my virginal womanhood. He probed my full pussy lips, opening up my soft folds and making me squirm. I kept sucking his hardening cock, my searching mouth moving up and down his throbbing instrument. It got harder to take care of his still rising rod. I was distracted as his fervent licking of my needy slit, became more intense. Multi-tasking was not my strong suit then so at times I stopped. When his penetrating tongue slid far into my hole, my pussy was soaked. I was pretty quiet despite the immense delight. I was not a screamer then. Not to mention, his parents were sleeping next door. I hoped they couldn't hear us. I will never know if they did.

After he had licked me to his heart's content and mine, he got on top of me and spread my legs and entered my starving love canal. He penetrated me slowly and outside of one quick jab of pain, his rapid thrusts in and out of my drenched pussy made me hotter and hotter. By the time we were done, the sheets had a touch of blood as a souvenir of what I no longer was. I had become a woman.

John left me right after we made love that night. He had no choice but to return to his room so that his parents wouldn't get suspicious. With a quick kiss, he left. I wished he would spend the night with me but understood why he couldn't.

I returned home to my parents in Montreal and continued with my education. John stayed in Ottawa and studied for his engineering degree; I earned my B.Comm. in computers from McGill University. We saw each other as often as we could on weekends and holidays. Some of the best moments of my life were during those visits.

Typically, I met him at the bus station and we went straight to the downtown hotel he always stayed at. Dinner could wait but our hunger for each other couldn't. We'd enter the hotel elevator and pretend to not know each other, unless we were the only two in it. I had my reputation to uphold, after all. I didn't want anyone to know that deep within this "good girl" was a "bad girl" dying to get out. The ride up to our floor seemed to take forever. I couldn't wait to have him hold me and touch me and to feel his prick enter me once again.

Shortly after entering the hotel room, I stood by the huge window with the curtains partly opened. The darkness of the room lit dimly, from the spectacular cityscape outside. John took me in his arms and we ardently kissed. His deep lingering kisses titillated my body. I needed him to take me then and there. If I had my way, he'd have thrown me onto the bed, ripped open my clothes with wanton abandon and made mad passionate love to me.

John instead carefully unbuttoned my shirt and expertly unhooked my bra. Then, he moved behind me. I took off my blouse and flung it onto the floor. My aroused body was eager to have his hands all over me. John quickly got undressed. He knew that nibbling on the side of my neck with his bare chest pressed against my back, turned the flicker in my hot pussy into a flaming passion. His moving fingers groped at my excited tits, reaching for them beneath the bra that still held them captive. He helped remove my brassiere and held onto my bountiful breasts, caressing my firm nipples tenderly.

John turned me around to face him and our wanting lips locked together. Our eager tongues danced in unison as our adventurous hands continued its exploration. I reached out and slowly stroked his thriving member; it grew quickly under my loving touch.

I got down on my knees and lustfully sucked on his pulsing rod. My head moved up and down his flourishing shaft and over his purple swollen cockhead. I looked up into his eyes and watched how he enjoyed the experience of my lips all over his expanding instrument. I deliberately pulled his booming dick out of my warm mouth and licked every inch of its tip, including fastidiously circling his piss hole.

With supersonic speed, he pulled me up and stripped me of the rest of my garments. John led me to our love spot on the bed. I'd lie on the bed and after another lingering kiss, he'd slowly move down to between my thighs. He positioned himself for what he told me was what he loved to do best, eat my sweet pussy.

John's searching tongue went into every part of my inviting folds of womanhood. He softly bit on my luscious lips. The more I squirmed with delight, the deeper his diving tongue went into my wet hole. My soft moans still not equal to the brewing excitement within me. His determined tongue moved back and forth into my moistened slit until I couldn't take it any longer. My overwhelming need to have his prick inside my starving cunt overtook my body.

"Fuck me," I begged.

"How badly do you want it, baby?" he'd teasingly ask.

"Please fuck me, John. I need it NOW."

John quickly sprang into action. He went to his pants and removed a rubber. He placed his condom on his ready instrument. He liked missionary style and I didn't know about the other positions. It felt so damn good that I wouldn't have cared anyhow.

He spread my legs wide and his erect dick slammed into my lusting pussy. He rapidly pumped his stiff pole repeatedly in and out of my tight cunt. He rhythmically thrust inside my titillated twat until his sperm emptied into his safe. We'd end up falling asleep in each other's arms. Later we woke up and went out to eat at some weird hour during the night. Thank heavens Montreal restaurants were open so late or we would have starved.

John and I had many romantic times together over the course of our 7-year relationship. We took a weekend trip to Quebec City one summer. He drove, holding my warm left hand almost the whole time. We got in at night and stayed in the first motel we could find. Not exactly 5 star accommodations but when you're young and in love, it doesn't matter.

The walls were paper thin and just like we could hear the talking from next door, I'm sure they heard us making love on that squeaky bed. My parents thought I was in Ottawa with my boyfriend and his parents but we required some alone time.

My career hit several roadblocks. My first full-time job turned into a disaster. I always had bad timing. I started in Dec at their busiest time of the year and that led to problems including tax issues. Their payroll dept clerk threatened me. He said they would ruin my career if I looked into my tax matter. I was young and naïve and trusted everyone. I made an unwise decision listening to my boss, when he agreed with me pursuing it. I had turned to him for advice. It was the biggest mistake of my life. The company was taken over and thousands of people lost their jobs including me.

I looked for a new job and came very close to getting one on several occasions but didn't get them. I couldn't understand why I never got the positions I applied for. That is, until one guy did me a favor and told me that I was being shafted by my ex boss. He said my previous company was clearly afraid of a lawsuit so he never actually said anything bad but nothing good either. It was enough to make sure I wouldn't get a job. In essence, I was blacklisted or blackballed or whatever it's called, from working in computers. I decided to switch fields into accounting.

I went back to McGill University and ended up with a degree in accounting. While completing this phase of my education, I found an accounting clerk job that I knew I couldn't keep once the winter set in. Montreal winters are quite brutal and since there was no bus that went right to my work, I had to walk quite a bit. I didn't know how to drive and the low-paying job wouldn't have allowed me to afford a car anyhow. I ended up slipping quite hard on the ice on my way to work one day and quit.

Ironically, the computer programmer there worked for my previous employer. On the day I resigned, my boss tried to get me to stay but I couldn't. It was then that he told me something that shocked me. Turns out my previous employer committed fraud and due to the tax issue I had, they blamed me for getting fined millions of dollars. I had no knowledge of what they had done. It ended up being a regular spot check the government randomly does so they were mistaken to think I had anything to do with their being caught. Regardless, that was why they decided to blackball me. It was good I switched careers.

I looked for a job again but it became increasingly harder since Quebec required employees to be bilingual or have a French name. My French was fine but I wasn't bilingual by any stretch. I ended up finding work in an accounting firm as an auditor.

Again, timing is everything and I have never had good timing. The company ended up getting rid of all junior accountants who weren't bilingual. That was Quebec. Hindsight is 20/20 but what I should have done is take my money and move to Toronto but I wasn't confident enough. Most young Anglophones, as English Quebecers were called, moved out of Quebec. I stayed and the gap in my resume grew bigger and bigger.

I decided to earn a professional accounting designation and did so on the first try. I just needed to complete my 2-years working requirement. During this time, John earned his engineering degree and moved to Toronto and later Montreal to be near me. I visited him in Toronto on several occasions. He lived in the lower part of a house. Not beautiful but having him for the whole weekend was wonderful. We made love on his bed.

Saying goodbye on each trip almost killed me. I cried at the bus depot and was upset each time for days. I couldn't bare being apart from him. When he moved to Montreal, I was ecstatic. The problem we had was that John asked me to marry him several times. I told him that I would never be able to marry him, when we first started dating. He felt I would change my mind. I didn't have the strength to lose my parents in the process. They warned me that if I married him, they no longer would see me. By the time he was 31, he really felt he had to find someone else. I was heartbroken but understood.

I wish things were handled differently though. We had broken off several times over the marriage issue and during one of our off times, he called in sick at work. I went to his apartment to nurse him back to health. I had a bad feeling in the pit of my stomach, as I headed to his unit. When I got there, I heard him and a woman. I couldn't make out all that was happening but I knew it wasn't good. I knocked on his door and in a little while after knocking again, a slip of paper was passed to me from underneath it. It was the most hurtful thing that had ever happened to me. It was written from the woman he was with. It said, "Get lost bitch. We're busy fucking." The pain I felt was beyond description. I felt betrayed that not only was my boyfriend of 7 years with another woman but he let her write me such a nasty letter.

John and I spoke a day or two later. I asked him how he could have let her send me that letter. He admitted he shouldn't have. He said he had been seeing her in Ottawa for a couple of months, when he went there to visit his parents. He told me he was moving back there. I asked him why he would choose her and he said he wanted me but since he was never going to have me, he had to move on. I understood. It hurt like hell but I didn't want to hold him back from finding someone he could marry. I just didn't like that he would choose a woman with no compassion. I would never have done what she did, not even to my worst enemy.

My sister ended up getting a job in Toronto and her relocation was paid. It was my one chance to move to an English speaking province and I took it. We came to Toronto in August 1994. I tried to get a job and couldn't. My resume was far from impressive due to all the unemployment I had. They didn't care about the bilingual issues in Quebec that affected my resume.

My sister's job contract came to an end a year or so later and together we decided to open up a dating service. It was specialized for BBW (Big Beautiful Women). We made a decision to go the classy route. We didn't want to advertise in sleazy magazines or anything like that. Everything we did was professional, from the business cards all the way to the contracts that were drawn up. We attracted and signed up some terrific women, many of them highly educated with great jobs. They just hadn't found the right guys.

During this time my sister found out about another position. Despite agreeing to do the business together, she bailed out a few months into our endeavor. She decided she preferred working for someone and getting a regular salary. She still remained a partner with me but wasn't really willing to take risks by investing in our company. It takes money to make money in that line of work and there just wasn't enough without her investing with me. It was doomed for failure. We had a second issue that prevented us from succeeding. Married men called to join our service but we refused. We didn't want to set up affairs. Our goal was to have our members get married. One couple in fact, did. Several couples did date for years. Others I have no idea. We also opened up a social club. Many members joined both our dating service and social club. We arranged events at various venues in Toronto, restaurants and comedy shows and anywhere else we could think of where people could become friends/lovers.

Despite features about us in The Toronto Star and The Sun and other local papers, as well as a mention by Mordechai Richler, which was the ultimate compliment, we decided to close down. We didn't file bankruptcy since we were never in debt. We just didn't earn enough money. Besides the one couple that married and the others that dated, the one positive thing that did come from it for me was, completing my job requirement for my professional accounting designation. Not that I use it in any way. Phone sex operators don't require accounting designations.

Here I was with no job so I started looking for one yet again. This was an odd experience. I kept getting controller level job interviews. I was really only a junior in accounting since owning the dating service involved doing everything like marketing and interviewing and admin and bookkeeping. Nothing that would make me qualified to be the head of accounting. I remember one company gave me a budgeting test and really liked me. I did great in the test, they told me at the interview. Unfortunately, my honesty lost me that job. They asked me how many years I did budgeting and I told them I hadn't done it at all at work. I should have told them 10 years. I would have been working as the head of their company.

I couldn't get a job. I was too educated but my working experience didn't match. I tried to convince companies I would be fine at a clerk position but was told repeatedly that I would never be satisfied there. I grew to dislike the word "overqualified" that I regularly was told. They didn't want to hire me and then have me leave on them. Nothing I said could talk them into it. I was pretty discouraged and I needed to earn a living.

Now this may be hard to believe but after John, I didn't really want another love interest. I always considered myself a one-man woman and John was that man. I didn't want to get hurt again either. There was a guy in Montreal, at my previous accounting clerk job. He kept staring at me. I actually didn't like it. Eventually he asked me out and I refused. Again, I wasn't interested in dating.

Years later, when I ran our dating service and social club from my home, I didn't really meet any men except when I interviewed them to become members. I wasn't about to mix business with pleasure anyhow. With all that was going on with my career, my focus was on everything but men. I didn't look for a man or think about one. I didn't even get horny except a few days a year. That is, while I was awake. When I slept, it was a different story. I had the wildest sex dreams imaginable. Denzel Washington was my favorite guest star in my sleep. I woke up many a night and had no doubt that I masturbated during my sleep. My fingers had the aroma from my pussy juices on them.

One day I was looking for a job on the computer. I received an e-mail that changed my life. It was a link to an erotic site and I saw a short sex clip. I watched it and my whole body reacted to what I saw. I was hot and bothered, after not having been with a man for 20 years. Time really does fly. My sexual side was reawakened to the millionth degree. I started searching the internet, on a mission to find more sex videos. I downloaded all I could find. This went on for days. My horniness grew rapidly and all I could think of was sex.

It was Dec 2002 that I discovered the joys of internet chatting. MSN Messenger, to be exact. I was obsessed with it. I was 44 years old and had only been with one guy my entire life. All I could think about was getting back on the computer. I slept only 2 – 4 hours a night and took very little time to eat food. I was instant messaging all the time, having cyber sex with men from all over the world. I was totally hooked.

I had never even said words like cunt prior to that and here I was saying things like "I am putting your cock in my mouth and taking it down really deep and..." I had become someone I didn't recognize, almost overnight. I even had a cyber gangbang. I was having cyber sex with a guy and another asked for an invite and then another and another. I can't recall how many men but I was the only woman taking care of all of them. I learned one thing. Gangbangs should be done in person. It was really hard to keep track of what each guy was doing to me and me to them. Shy Elaine was gone forever, at least online.

I found out about an adult website and joined that also. It was there that I met men so that I could have more sexual conversations. I was addicted to it by this point. I watched more erotic clips and I wanted to fuck but I wasn't ready to take that step. Cyber would have to do. I became online friends with quite a few guys on that site.

There was an older guy that I chatted with many times daily. When we met, after he convinced me that friendship would be fine, it was clear he was out for only one thing from me and it wasn't to be friends. When we sat at a table, he rubbed one of his legs all along mine. My pussy was throbbing for some attention. I still refused him when he asked to have sex. It was too soon but I was very tempted.

I continued chatting with men on MSN and guys from that adult site. At MSN I met a man, a much older man. He was the filthiest, most disgusting man that I had ever spoken to, in person or online.

He said he cared about me and I desperately needed some loving attention. We had cyber sex all the time it seemed. We did it morning, midday and night on a daily basis. I used to sit at my computer desk, spread my legs and move my fingers in and out of my pussy. He was crude, very crude. He called me slut and whore and instead of being turned off, it made me want to talk to him more. "Suck my cock, slut," he'd say and I would tell him how I was doing it to him. I couldn't get enough of it.

Besides that dirty old man, there were many others. There was an Italian guy that really turned me on. He always ate my pussy out first. I chatted with 100s of men. I couldn't keep track.

The first guy I decided to meet in person was married. I'm not proud of that fact but it's the truth. He had a date to have sex with another woman so I felt that he would be cheating with or without me. I spoke to some friends and they felt I should be with a married man, for my first experience post John. It was their belief that I would get hooked on the first guy that touched me, after not having sex for so long. They thought that a married man would be unavailable so that would be best. That made some sense. I never felt a woman should be with a married man but there I was.

Aaron and I met at a coffee shop and we both knew why we were there. We were both a bit awkward about it but we came back to my house. Aaron felt guilty about cheating on his wife but only when it came to fucking but not sucking. I will never really understand that. He put his dick in me for a second and removed it. He felt guilty like sin about his wife and about me. He said it was because I was single so he felt like he was hurting me too. I never quite got that part either.

Aaron loved how I sucked his cock. He said I was the best cocksucker he ever had. I asked how that was possible given I only sucked my boyfriend before him and he said it must be a natural talent. It amazed me how much I loved eagerly taking his throbbing dick in my mouth and feeling it expand. Aaron was a groaner and the more he groaned, the more passion I had for his hot rod. It surprised me how much I had changed since John. I don't know if it was because I hadn't had a prick in my mouth for so long but I was not the same girl who didn't care if I gave a blowjob or not. I longed to give Aaron fellatio. I made sure I licked his prick thoroughly and gave it my all. He blew a load in my mouth with an explosive force that only added to the excitement of drinking his cum.

Aaron was wonderful at oral sex. He licked my swollen cunt with his long tongue and my moans were no longer low. I verbalized my immense pleasure at his talents, which he bestowed on my pussy and later ass. Getting me to let him lick my behind was not an easy task. I was the same woman that didn't even let her ex boyfriend see her rear, let alone bury his tongue inside it. I was so glad Aaron talked me into it. His tongue moved wildly inside my butt hole and noises came out of my mouth that I didn't recognize. It was amazing how wonderful his touring of my most private place felt.

Aaron couldn't see me often due to his work and his wife. In fact, I believe we only ended up seeing each other on 4 occasions over a 6 months period. It was during this time that I met a guy at the same site as Aaron. He really turned me on. He wrote me a message and something in his profile was very intriguing. I looked at his photo and he was black and that had no bearing. I gave him my contact info. One early morning around midnight, he wrote me an instant message. It was love at first site; at least that's how I felt. Steve and I chatted for 6 hours straight, stopping only for short visits to the washroom. I felt sparks over the computer. In all honesty, I felt more for him that first day than I did for John in the 7 years we were together. I know that's hard to believe but it's true. Steve only left our first chat since he had an appointment at work.

I went to bed and he had sent me a message with a virtual rose. He echoed my feelings for him. He didn't say love or anything like that but it was clear that he felt a lot. He said he never felt so much so quickly. I was on a high for a couple of days. It sure seemed like I was in love. I never met him in person. I knew it made no sense but try telling my heart that.

When I saw Steve's popup on MSN, my heart did a pitter-patter. Reality then reared its ugly head. I fell asleep one day and hadn't logged out of MSN. I woke up to find an instant message from Steve. It was a nasty message saying that I ignored his messages and put myself on away to talk to other men. He no longer was going to chat with me. I couldn't figure out why he thought that. When he came on, I always went right to him no matter who I was speaking with. I finally figured out what happened. MSN automatically put me on "away" status after 15 minutes of inactivity. I had been sleeping but when Steve came on he saw me listed as "available" and since my timing sucked as usual, it then went to "away". Steve thought I was around to put it to "away" and that it was so I could talk to others instead of to him. He jumped to the wrong conclusion. I was determined to get him back. I sent him e-mails explaining what happened but it didn't help. He had a very jealous nature. It literally took days to get him to forgive me for something I never did.

Steve and I would make up and then he'd get mad about other perceived things involving other men. He was wrong about each matter and he became very insulting when angry. I hyperventilated on several occasions as a result. He didn't like me talking to the older dirty nasty man or seeing Aaron. I had invited him to come visit me and stay at my home, which is something I never would have done with anyone else I met online. I was that hooked on him.

When we had one of our fights, they usually involved those 2 other men, he suddenly moved to another State. He decided a woman he met online before me, would be his new live-in girlfriend. He moved into her home. I was extremely shocked and hurt.

I didn't believe he cared more for his new girlfriend than he did for me. Two reasons supported my opinion. One, on the way to move in with her, he called me. I had given him my phone number and here he was on the way to her and he was phoning me. He was listening to my favorite song. He had asked me what song I liked best during one of our chats and he liked it too. He was playing that song. Secondly, when she would wait for him to make love to her, he often would instead be chatting online with me. She'd fall asleep while we talked for hours daily online.

The dirty old man lost some of his power on me but he still had some. He actually tried to get me to start hooking on the streets and that he should be sent my earnings. There was no chance of that. First, there was no way I was going to become a prostitute. Second, if I worked as one, my earnings would be mine not his. I was an accountant after all. What he wanted would never happen. I laughed it off.

One day he went a little too far. I purchased a web cam at a great price. The sale was so good that my family bought several as gifts and I bought one for myself. During one of our chats, I made the mistake of telling him I now owned a cam. He told me to put it on. As usual, I took orders from him.

"Unbutton your blouse," he demanded. I didn't want to so I hesitated. "I told you, unbutton your blouse. Do it." I could tell he was getting angry.

"Ok, it's unbuttoned," I replied, after they were all opened.

"Take off your shirt," he continued.

"Ok but I'm keeping my bra on," I stated.

"Fine," he said.

I stood in front of my web cam, knowing he was staring at me. It made me feel very uneasy.

"Now take off your bra. I want to see your big tits," he insisted.

"Please don't make me take off my bra. You know I said I won't," I begged.

"Do it whore and shut up," he commanded.

I unclipped my bra and hesitantly removed it from my large breasts. Instead of on me, covering up my 40DD tits like I preferred, my brassiere was placed on the bed beside the computer in my bedroom. I felt uncomfortable being so exposed to this man. I could feel him leering at me even though I couldn't see him back. He didn't have a cam. Worse than that, I felt like the cheap whore he called me.

"Take off the rest of your clothes. I want to see your whole body," he bellowed.

" No.........please... I don't want to," I stammered.

"Shut up and do it, slut."

There was no reasoning with him. My feelings meant nothing to him. I did as instructed. I was stark naked for him to see. He had me move around so he could see my ass. My discomfort level rose, as I turned around to show it to him.

"Very nice, bitch. Thank you." He was pleased. He knew I'm a BBW from my picture and liked that.

I was about to get dressed again when he heard my sister in the background. He had recently told me some stories, which I wasn't sure whether or not to believe. He had told me that he had slept with both his mother and his sister. Suddenly, a new idea evolved in his nasty mind.

"Tell your sister to come in here. I want to watch you licking her cunt." That was it. That was the last straw. I closed my web cam and closed down my MSN and sent him an e-mail saying I was through with him. He went too far.

I was very upset with myself for showing him my body. I can't explain why I did this but when I chatted with some online friends later that day, I felt so horrible about myself that I asked them if they'd like to see me naked. They all said yes. I showed myself to probably 5 or 6 men that day and the next. That was only the beginning. My online "friends" asked me to do things on the cam for them.

"Lick your nipples," was a popular request.

"Use your dildo and fuck your pussy."

I resisted at first. Then I thought I'm naked anyhow. I performed for them like an adult circus act without the acrobatics. I improvised too. Men loved when I took my dildo and sucked it like I was cocksucking their pricks. Placement of the web cam was key and I became a master at placing it exactly right. I spread my legs and used my 10-inch thick dildo, moving it into my wet cunt while they eagerly watched. The men wrote messages to me like:

"That's it Elaine, stick it in deeper,"

"How deep could you shove that dildo in?"

"Play with your cunt with your fingers. Let me hear your wetness."

"Put the cam closer to your pussy. I want to see your lips."

I actually broke my first cam because it fell too often, when I moved the cam towards my puffed slit for those close-ups. I heard it all. I would show myself to these men and it made me feel good and bad at the same time. They loved my body and honestly, I needed to hear that. I couldn't believe they felt that way. Yes, the odd man didn't want to see a plus sized woman but that only happened a few times. There was a cute young guy who used to write me every night, to see me on cam before he went to bed. Just looking at my tits made him cum. I'd be lying if I said I wasn't flattered by the attention.

I got in the habit of letting many men watch at the same time. Men I knew from chatting but still strangers in most respects. Some nights, I played to probably about 6 men at a session. The more men that watched me, the more excited I was. I moaned using my fingers or dildo and later my silver bullet. I put on quite the show. Some had me watch them on their cams. They stroked their limp cocks for me until they were erect. They'd blow a load; their sperm covered their fingers. I used to fantasize about fucking myself on a cam site that had no maximum viewers unlike messenger. In my imagination, I would watch the number of viewers increase as I performed. Sometimes I still masturbate to that thought.

Steve eventually broke off with his girlfriend and moved back to Chicago. He never let me cam for him. He said he didn't want to be like all the other men I chatted with. He saw my face on the cam once or twice but he never saw me naked. Steve was the reason I got interested in erotic stories. He wrote them and when he gave me a few of his to read, I was turned on immensely. He needed a proofreader and I volunteered my time to help him. Payment was getting to be the first to read his words. We spent time going over all the comments I made and he seemed to be very glad I did.

When I first met Steve, he said that if a woman inspired him to write a story involving her that would indicate he felt strongly about the woman. He decided to write a story about me and I was on cloud 9. I still keep it in my drawer. On my birthday, Steve contacted me at 12am sharp, letting me know he cared enough to be the first to wish me Happy Birthday. He sent me a gift too. Both heartfelt actions touched me.

Steve told me that he would never meet me in person. His reason seemed to be about Aaron. He didn't like that I accepted being treated so badly, not getting fucked only sucked. Not to mention the cancelled dates, when Aaron had to work. Steve always acted like whoever he was meeting with in person was real and that we were online only. I believed he would never meet me so I did go out with other men. Going out might not be the correct way of phrasing it. Getting fucked or sucking men would be more accurate. It's like a person that is dying of thirst. They would probably over drink. After no sex for 20 years, I hungered for as much of it as I could get. My story Irresistible Temptations was the only other story I wrote with quite a bit of truth to it. I really did meet that stranger, only he didn't have that accent and the ending was fabricated. We did fuck at my house and my mom was home. It was great spontaneous sex.

I met one guy during the night. Not a smart thing to do but I did it anyhow. I walked to our arranged meeting place and ended up in his van to keep warm. He opened my blouse and I closed it. That kept happening until eventually he got his way. He fondled my tits. Then he pulled out his cock and began playing with it. I wasn't interested in doing anything but he pulled the seat back and begged me to put my mouth on it. I said no and he pleaded some more. I knew he would win and I was tired so I placed my mouth on his dick and sucked for a minute only. He shook like a leaf and shot a load of hot cum in my mouth. Then he zipped up his fly and took me home.

Aaron ended up leaving me to fuck another woman. That lasted a very short time and since then he's asked to be with me again but I've refused. It's fun to chat with him online to this day but deep down I think he knows it won't ever happen.

I have been with other married men and single men since Aaron. There was a married guy who hadn't had sex with his wife in 5 years and he was supposed to be a friend only. He came over and brought me a present and one thing led to another. We ended up fucking. I liked him as a person but sexually, I didn't really care to be intimate with him. His dick was very tiny and he used to say that was a problem for him with women. I broke it off with him but not just because of his cock size.

Another married guy came over as a friend, one day that I needed a friend. We had an arrangement that he wouldn't touch me unless I initiated it. He didn't keep his word. I was wearing my nightgown and housecoat since it was early in the morning. Before I knew it, he was on the floor and started eating my pussy. It's very hard to tell a guy to leave, when your wet cunt is dying for more attention and your loud moans aren't hiding the enjoyment you're experiencing.

Jeff was one of the most oral guys I had been with. It was amazing but every short while he would tell me to squat over his face so he could eat my pussy more. He stuck his exploring tongue deep inside my folds and buried it in my hot cunt. I didn't see him again because I talked him into trying harder with his wife. When we chatted many months later, he said that I gave him back his sexual confidence. He told me things went well with his spouse for a short time but eventually it failed again.

There were 2 other married men I had been with. One was a total mistake. I knew immediately it was so I sucked his cock but we didn't fuck. I didn't even really want to do that. The other married man was different. I really liked Derrick and actually still do, as a friend. He's an Indian man with an accounting designation. When we chatted online for the first time, we finished each other's sentences. I was amazed. Intellectually, we were equals.

Derrick and his wife hadn't had sex since she gave him a "Christmas present" about 9 months before. He told me that he hoped she'd catch us having lunch. He said he was thinking about filing for divorce. I believed it. He wished to take me out as a friend so I agreed. His online picture didn't turn me on but in person, he did immediately. He felt the same about me, I found out later. We had lunch and he took me home. He asked to give me a quick kiss. I agreed. Later on, I found out that he thought I wasn't interested and he was disappointed. We talked online and found out that it was a mutual attraction.

Derrick and I saw each other when we could. He was the first one that fucked my ass. To this day, he talks about how he once jumped on the kitchen counter and I sucked him so good and deep. I enjoyed Derrick on many levels because he stimulated my mind first before my body. He was my friend and my lover. He ended up getting the flu and his wife suddenly remembered he was alive. They got closer and ended up fucking like rabbits, day and night. We stopped seeing each other since if a marriage could be saved, that should always come first. That was the last I saw of Derrick. We still chat. His marriage was great for a bit and then reverted back to sex being rare. He requested seeing me again but by that time, I refused.

I never tried to break up any marriages and the men I had sex with were those who were actively looking to cheat. Derrick cheated before meeting me and since his marriage took a turn for the worse, did so again. In fact, they all did. You might not believe this but I would never cheat. I didn't cheat on my first boyfriend and I wouldn't on my present one. Again I'm not proud of it but I felt that my real life story should be true. The Elaine of today would not see a married man, period.

The single men I met weren't married but they used me just the same. The men were different but the scenarios were similar. There was one guy that I really liked. His name is Guy. He's an architect and I was crazy about him. He was a player but was upfront about it. I really like that. I remember our first date. I refused to have sex with him. Men will never understand this but if a woman really likes a guy and wants a future with him, she most likely won't fuck him until the 3rd date. If she doesn't want him, first dates are fine. We went to a movie. Guy loves going to the cinema. During the movie, Guy's wandering hands were all over my body. He didn't stick his fingers inside my pussy but he sure made my panties wet. When the movie ended, everyone left. That is, everyone but us. As I got up to leave, he began touching me all over. I was aroused and flattered but I knew we had to go. We left and he asked me out the next night.

We ended up at his place the following evening and what I've learned is that when I go to Guy's house to "watch a movie", we never end up watching it all. We start viewing it and after a short while, Guy gets down on his knees and after pulling down my panties and moving everything else out of the way, his tongue is in my aroused cunt. Before I know it, we are headed for his bedroom. Guy literally would look at my slit for an hour or longer and finger it.

On our first sexual encounter, Guy couldn't find a condom so we had 6 hours of foreplay. I sucked on his dick on and off, taking it down my throat and he kept licking the moist area between my thighs. When he took me home, we arranged to see each again in a couple of days.

It was very similar to the first time. Movie in and pretty soon, there he was on his knees licking my juicy cunt. Off he led me into the bedroom but this time he was prepared. He wasn't about to not get to fuck this time.

"Ride my cock, baby," Guy told me.

I squatted on top of him and found the position above his throbbing dick. I slid down his hard prick all the way down to his balls. He liked touching my bouncing tits as I moved up and down his manhood.

"God that feels sooooooo good," he groaned loudly. He was the most vocal man I had ever been with.

He started thrusting his erect rod inside me as I fucked him. That added to our pleasure. He fondled my firm nipples and lay back and enjoyed himself until he shot his sperm into the condom. He cleaned himself and got dressed again and took me home. I didn't really like that part. I hoped to stay longer. I knew that after the act, that wasn't really what Guy desired. He told me he wasn't looking for a relationship, having been burnt by catching his wife cheating on him. They divorced.

Steve didn't like me seeing any of the men I did. He especially didn't like my fondness for Guy. I had my house to myself one weekend, while my sister went away. I said it in passing to Steve and arranged to see Guy at my house instead of his, for a change. Little did I know that despite the fact that Steve always made it clear that we were just online friends and he would never see me in person, he booked a plane to come see me.

We talked on the phone and I said about my plan to see Guy, not knowing he booked his trip. He flipped out on the phone and told me the arrangements he made.

"I didn't know you were planning to come see me. You said you never would," I explained.

"Forget it. I'm canceling my plans," he shot back.

"Please Steve, you know that you're the one I want. I'll cancel Guy," I pleaded. I knew Guy wouldn't really care.

"Don't bother, I'm not coming now or ever," Steve retorted.

Steve was true to his word. Things were never the same after that. He started seeing other women. A few times I thought he was in love until things fell through and he would be with the next one. That is, until he found Sue. He later let me know that it was a site I introduced him to inadvertently years before. I said it in passing that I joined it and between women he signed up and found Sue. They got married a little over a year ago and we rarely chat. I miss his friendship and wish him the best and he knows that.

Even though I did see men, I was often alone. I decided to join Lavalife by phone. I met some guys there that are still friends of mine. We talked on the phone but no sex. Some online contacts asked me about doing phone sex with them but I couldn't. I was too shy. I gave in to some on one condition. I would listen to them playing with themselves but I wouldn't reciprocate. How could I moan for a stranger? I said things to them over the phone like I did in cyber sex. Only this time, I heard their voices and when they came from me telling them what I would do to their pricks, I loved hearing them orgasm.

I still couldn't get past the idea of me touching myself, while a stranger listens. That is, until one guy coaxed me into using my toy. He didn't have me say much. He told me that it was for my pleasure only. He just said I should relax and enjoy myself.

"Take your egg (my then favorite toy) and rub it on your clit," he instructed.

He could hear the vibrating toy perform. I involuntarily moaned as I used it on my swelling clit. The more I moaned, the more I could hear his breathing deepen.

"That's it, now take your dildo and stick it deep in your cunt," he continued.

I could tell that he was on the verge of cumming. My 10-inch tool did its job and I pushed it in slowly. My welcoming pussy widened to accommodate its girth. My energized moans got stronger. I no longer cared about who was listening to me pleasuring myself. I was lost in my lust.

Then it happened, the moment that changed my life. It wasn't just that he shot his load. I heard men cum before. It was that he came from hearing me. He didn't want to have an orgasm. He was embarrassed and kept apologizing.

"Oh god, I'm so sorry. I didn't want to cum. This was supposed to be for you," he stammered.

"I heard you moaning and I don't know…. I came," he explained.

I could tell his words weren't hollow. He couldn't help cumming. It excited me knowing that just hearing me moan could make a man cum. I stopped doing cyber sex, which had become too routine and instead my focus shifted to phone sex.

There was a man that I started doing it with. His name was Gord and we had phone sex sessions typically lasting 2 hours. It was Gord that I credit with making me realize how much I loved gangbangs and how pleasurable phone sex could be. In one of our best phone calls, we did a scenario with me being brought to a cabin. There were 25 guys waiting for me. I knew that by the end of that weekend, every single guy in that room would have fucked me several times. I was tied up on a bed and serviced them all. During that call, I felt like they had all plunged their growing dicks into my insatiable slit. I felt like cum was dripping out of my mouth from sucking all their pricks and of course, some just sprayed their loads over my body. I was in heaven. Seriously, it was better than some of the real sex I had by that point.

I had sizzling hot phone sex with several guys and enjoyed it immensely. The problem was that I really needed to earn a living. One phone fuck buddy suggested to me to do phone sex for a living. I made him cum 4 times the first time we did it and from then only, a minimum of 2-3 times each time we had it. He said I'm good so why shouldn't I get paid for it since I need the money. I laughed it off at first. Then I thought about it and spoke to Gord and some others. They all said I should do it.

I did need the money and why not do what I enjoy and get paid for it? My sister didn't like the idea but since she doesn't pay for my upkeep, I needed to earn money. My mind was made up. I would be a phone sex operator. Easier said than done. I live in Canada and it's not like in the USA. It's not that easy to find phone sex jobs. I researched on the internet and finally found one. I worked for my boss for 5 years but we recently parted ways.

I now work for myself. So if you call to speak to someone in their 20s or 30s or 50s, you might be talking to me. We sell fantasies. The odd minority shows their real pics because they work on a cam. The great majority of phone sex operators aren't what their pics show. However, the stereotype PSO (phone sex operator) is not true, at least it isn't in my case. I do not sit and do other things, while I pretend to be horny talking to my clients.

I lie down on my bed and I have a magic wand toy I use. The wand took over as my favorite toy. Its intensity on my pussy is beyond compare to anything except my fucking machine. Last year, I added to my collection of rabbits (sex toy) and eggs and magic wands and dildos. I bought a fucking machine. It could thrust into my pussy up to 268 strokes per minute and I love when my current boyfriend relaxes during sex and the machine takes over. Then my boyfriend continues. Nothing beats a combo of real cock and deep fast fucking, at least not to me.

When I met my present boyfriend, he asked what I did to earn a living. He wasn't thrilled that I was a PSO. When we talked the next day and he had time to think things over, he was fine with it. He understood it was something I need to do. With time, he has grown to like when he is with me during a call. Several times he has eaten out my cunt while I made another man cum. Once I sucked his cock while the client listened and enjoyed and came too.

There is no way that I would give out any personal info on any client. I wouldn't give it to my boyfriend, sister or to anyone else. It's confidential. What I will tell is that many men have fantasized about fucking their mothers. I don't know if it began with breastfeeding. Perhaps when you start off life with sucking your mom's tits, it's inevitable. Father/daughter fantasies are also pretty common. Their daughters are always young and virginal and they want to be the first man to fill their pussies.

Phone sex scenarios are not real so why people get upset by them, shocks me. Women fantasize about rape but do we want to get raped for real? NO. I don't promote anything illegal not now or ever. I don't care what you dream about doing but I would care deeply if you actually did it.

I have worked for several companies doing phone sex. One of them I did for one day. It really sucked. NO pun intended. That job fit the stereotype. I had to lie in bed with the phone next to me, ready to answer. Of course, no calls equals no pay. You only get paid for calls you do. That is usual for all phone sex jobs. The difference here was that I had to wait for calls. I couldn't generate any. Worse yet, it was beyond boring waiting for a call and we were told to talk about anything but sex to keep them on longer. Now, I don't know about you but if I was a man calling in for phone sex, I damn well better get my cock sucked and fucked. We weren't supposed to give them pleasure. We were supposed to talk about the weather and anything else to keep them talking. I quit.

When phone sex is no longer about making the men happy and them getting off, I don't want to do it. I worked at another company that had virtual sex. Ever had that? Virtual sex is having an avatar represent you. You go to a virtual room and virtually fuck or get your cock sucked or pussy licked. You see your avatars going at it. I was a "working girl" at one of those virtual reality sites. I was very popular because most of the women just clicked on a script during sex, choosing from a list what their avatar would say next. I actually typed things from my head, to give the most enjoyable experience I could. There was so much nonstop typing. It became too much work and guys spent too much money doing it with me. They said that with me, it felt real. I left there because it was out of control and way too much typing. It also began to bore me.

Most of the phone sex I do now is by blocks of time. I love getting to know a man better and getting a feel for what he is turned on by the most. My aim is to give him the most pleasurable experience I could. I look forward to hearing from my regulars and hearing them cum is my best reward. I want to have fun too so when I use my toys, I'm having a wonderful time. When the guy isn't participating, it isn't as much fun. Phone sex is like real sex, it's best when there's chemistry between the 2 parties.

After proofreading quite a few of Steve's stories and we drifted apart after what happened with Guy, I started dabbling with writing myself. A guy that used to call me from Ireland sent me a story he wrote and asked me to finish it. I did and he loved my ending. I had a great time doing it. Then I wrote a paragraph and showed it to a contact and he loved it. This is truly how my writing started. Here's that paragraph without any editing:

I am just imagining you ringing the bell and me yelling out come in. I am masturbating with my egg on the family room floor. You come in and start watching as I move my vibrating egg, speed 4, all along my pussy. Then, you watch as I start thrusting my 7-inch g spot vibrator in and out. Moaning as I do this. You have to taste my pussy, you want it sooooo much. You take the wet vibrator out and lick it. Then you start eating me as you tell me to use my egg on my clit. I am enjoying it and tell you as such with my louder moans. Then you tell me to rub my egg on the rest of my cunt. My clit is yours. You lick on it harder and suck it. I suck my nipples as you look up at me as you enjoy how my pussy tastes. Your cock is getting harder by my response. You want me to cum and I am getting closer and closer and............

I showed it to other contacts and they liked it too. I then wrote this and it too was well received:

Just a thought...

You watch as my sister leaves the house in a hurry, forgetting to lock the door in her haste. You seize the opportunity and let yourself in after she drives away. Making your way up the steps and into my bedroom, you see me seated in my chair at the computer, focused completely on what I am doing online. I don't hear you approach. You lower your body to lessen the chances of me noticing you and it works. Soon you are beneath my chair. I am relaxed with my legs slightly parted. Wearing only my nightgown, no panties or bra underneath, you look at my pussy. Enjoying the view you can't resist sticking your finger deep to probe my cunt. You add 2 more fingers since I need them, need them badly. Taking them out of my dripping pussy, you give me your fingers to suck and I taste good. You put your fingers back in and out, in and out. Then you remove them to taste me yourself. A smile on your face tells it all. I let out a gasp as you begin inserting your tongue deeper inside my very wet pussy. Seeing you below me, I push your head closer to the center of my increasing desire. My moans are getting more animated as you lick me faster and faster. You tell me to rub my clit as you continue fingering me and there is nothing I want more than to feel your cock inside me. You gently move my hand away from my clit so your mouth can get its rightful turn. Sucking on my swollen clit makes me moan all the more. Your cock is throbbing uncontrollably. You want to fuck me and can hardly contain yourself. You get up from the floor and get on top of me, pushing the chair, which is now leaning on the bed. Your thrusts are deep and both of us are enjoying fulfilling our hunger for each other.....

That's when I started writing full stories and posting them and that's "How I Became A Phone Sex Operator."

THE END

ABOUT THE AUTHOR:

Elaine Shuel has had a varied career. University educated, she has held several professional positions. Elaine has enjoyed using creativity to accomplish her goals. Writing erotic stories has been especially gratifying and challenging. She is the proud recipient of a 2010 Author Award at A1adultebooks. Elaine will continue surprising her readers with unexpected twists whenever possible.

Her work as a phone sex operator and erotic stories author, gives her the opportunity to stimulate both her readers and callers. Giving pleasure is her top priority and one she relishes doing.

Elaine feels that she has many facets to her personality that she likes to explore. While erotica gives her a chance to express her sexual side, she does enjoy writing about other topics that she has interest in. She has already written a fictional story for young adults called Mindy's Favorite Room. Ask Elaine is yet another book that is a departure from erotica. It is one she hopes will make a difference in someone's life, when making certain decisions. What means the most personally to Elaine, is her newest book Skippy, a fictional children's story written with the love she feels for her dog who died in 1988. He is forever in her heart.

ELAINE SHUEL ONLINE:

E-mail: **shuel_2000@yahoo.ca**

Yahoo Messenger: shuel_2000

MSN Messenger: **shuel2002@hotmail.com**

Website: **http://elaineshuel.com**

SOME OTHER ELAINE SHUEL BOOKS:

- **Simon Says**
- **Taught A Lesson**
- **Wide Open**
- **BDSM Tetralogy**
- **My Wife's A Gangbang Addict**
- **My Neighbour, The Nympho**
- **Taken For A Ride**
- **Caught In The Act**
- **Erotica Author Bares All**
- **The Surprise**
- **The Ins And Outs Of Becoming A Phone Sex Operator**
- **Women Who Love Black Meat**

19462338R00021

Printed in Poland
by Amazon Fulfillment
Poland Sp. z o.o., Wrocław